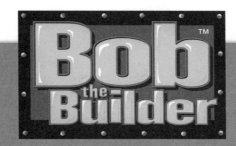

SNOWED UNDER

The BOBBLESBERG WINTER GAMES

SIMON SPOTLIGHT
New York   London   Toronto   Sydney

Based upon the television series *Bob the Builder*™ created by HIT Entertainment PLC and Keith Chapman, as seen on Nick Jr.® Photos by HOT Animation. Based on a script by Sarah Ball. Adapted by Wendy Wax.

SIMON SPOTLIGHT
An imprint of Simon & Schuster Children's Publishing Division
1230 Avenue of the Americas
New York, New York 10020

Manufactured in the United States of America

First Edition

2 4 6 8 10 9 7 5 3 1

ISBN 0-689-87141-4

It was a snowy night in Bobblesberg. Bob, Wendy, and Pilchard were sleeping in a hotel. Scoop, Muck, Dizzy, and Lofty were sound asleep in a garage. They had a busy day ahead of them.

"The mayor of Bobsville would like us to build her a log cabin," Bob told Scoop the next morning. "She needs a place to stay during the Winter Games. Will you be our team leader?"

"Sure, Bob," said Scoop. "I won't let you down!"

"Great," said Bob. He pulled out a map and pointed to the site. "I'll see you there."

"Hop on," Zoomer, the snowmobile, said to Bob.

"That's okay," said Scoop. "*I* always drive Bob around."

"But you don't have snow tracks like I do," said Zoomer.

"Zoomer is right," Bob said to Scoop. "It's safer for me to ride on him in all this snow." Scoop wasn't too happy.

"Wheee!" Bob squealed as they rode through town. They rode past houses, cafés, a bakery, and a skiwear shop. Then they went over a bridge and toward the slopes. Riding Zoomer was fun!

Meanwhile, Wendy was busy practicing for
the big ski race. The Bobsville ski team was going to race
against the Bobblesberg ski team in the Winter Games.
She jumped so high, she felt like she was flying.

Scoop rounded up Dizzy, Roley, Muck, and Lofty.

"Bob made me the team leader," Scoop said, trying to sound important. "We are going to build a log cabin for the mayor of Bobsville. We have no time to—"

"Excuse me," said a mini-machine that was hurrying toward them. He looked upset.

"I'm Benny," said the mini-machine. "I'm here to build things for the Winter Games, but my teammates are stuck in a blizzard. If the work doesn't get done, the games will be canceled. Can you help me?"

"Yes, we can!" said Scoop, without talking to the rest of his team.

"Why did you say yes, Scoop?" Muck asked.

"We don't know how to do the work Benny needs," said Dizzy.

"And Bob wants us to build the log cabin," said Lofty.

"He's expecting us any minute," said Roley.

"I said yes because *I'm* in charge," said Scoop. "If the ski jumps aren't made, Wendy won't be able to race. I know! The four of you can help Bob, and I can help Benny."

"What should we tell Bob?" asked Lofty.

"Tell him I'm doing something that will make him proud," said Scoop.

Bob was surprised to hear about Scoop, but he was too busy cutting down trees to think about it. While Muck cleared the site, Lofty carried the logs over.

Roley flattened the ground. When they were ready, Dizzy poured the concrete.

"Great work, team!" said Bob, climbing onto Zoomer. "Before we start on the roof, I'm going to check on Scoop."

Bob found Scoop making lumpy bumps called moguls. The racers would ski in the grooves between them on their way downhill.

"Nice work!" said Bob.

"Thanks," said Scoop, beaming with pride. He didn't tell Bob that Benny had done most of the work.

"We still have a lot of work to do," said Benny. "We're running out of time."

"Muck, Roley, and Dizzy can help you," said Bob, "while Lofty helps me finish the cabin."

"But we don't *need* them," said Scoop. He wanted to do everything himself.

"We need all the help we can get," said Benny. "We haven't even started on the ski jumps and the ice-skating rink."

Benny explained what had to be done. "Muck, I need you to smooth off the jumps. Put the extra snow in Dizzy's barrel, and she can tip it over the jump. Roley, I need you to flatten the snow in front of the jumps."

"But *I* want to do those jobs," said Scoop.

"Sorry, Scoop," said Benny, "but your teammates are better built for these jobs than you are. Make sure they do a good job."

Muck, Dizzy, and Roley began to work.

"Can we build it?" Muck shouted, dropping snow into Dizzy's barrel.

"Hey, I'm supposed to say that!" said Scoop. "I'm the team leader."

But no one heard him over the loud, **"Yes, we can!"**

"Quiet down!" Scoop shouted miserably.

Watching his teammates work gave Scoop an idea. "Muck, Roley, and Dizzy," he said, "we don't need you anymore. I can finish up."

"But Benny said . . ." said Roley.

"Benny's not your team leader," said Scoop. "*I* am."

Muck, Roley, and Dizzy wandered past skiers, snowboarders, and ice-skaters. Some were practicing for the Winter Games. Others were just having fun. When they came to the children's rink, Dizzy tried ice-skating for the first time!

"This is taking too long," Benny said to Scoop. "Where did your teammates go?"

"Uh . . . they had other stuff to do," said Scoop.

Bob came to check on them. "The log cabin is finished," he said. "How is—*where* is everybody?"

Scoop wished he hadn't sent the others away. He could have used their help.

Muck, Roley, and Dizzy found Benny staring at the unfinished rink.

"What a mess!" said Muck.

"We'll never have this ice rink ready for the Winter Games," said Benny.

"It's too bad Scoop didn't want to work as a team," said Roley.

"I think he was worried that Bob wouldn't be proud of him," said Dizzy.

Just then Bob, Zoomer, and Scoop appeared.

"Oh, no!" groaned Scoop when he saw the unfinished rink.

"We're here to help you, Scoop," Muck said.

Scoop was grateful. "I'm sorry for not being a very good team leader," he said.

"We forgive you," said Roley. **"Now, can we do it?"**

"Yes, we can!" they shouted.

At last it was time for the Winter Games. Bob, the machines, and the mayor of Bobsville watched as Wendy raced down the hill. Everyone cheered as she finished first. The Bobsville ski team beat the Bobblesberg ski team by one point!

Wendy wasn't the only one to get a gold medal. Lofty, Roley, Dizzy, Muck, and Scoop got them too.

"I'm proud to be a part of the best team in the world!" said Scoop. "We can fix anything, can't we?"

The team cheered, **"Yes, we can!"**